Mad About

Triceratops, T rex, Stegosaurus, and other dinosaurs

Stegosaurus
(STEG-owe-SORE-uss)

- lived around 155–144 million years ago
- 13 ft (4 m) tall

make believe ideas

This box shows you how to pronounce the dinosaur's name. It also shows you how big the dinosaur was and tells you when it lived.

This is the symbol for a meat-eating dinosaur.

This is the symbol for a plant-eating dinosaur.

Dinosaur experts learn more about dinosaurs every day. Although we cannot include future discoveries, we have tried to ensure that this book is as accurate as possible.

Tyrannosaurus rex

Tyrannosaurus rex was a fierce **meat eater**. It could crunch bones in its strong **jaw** and even swallow its food whole!

Little arms

T rex had such short **arms** that it couldn't even touch its nose!

sharp teeth..........

jaw closed

short arm

Mad about T rex

T rex had a bite that was six times stronger than that of a lion!

A hungry T rex could chomp its way through the equivalent of 1,500 sausages a day!

T rex was so large, it could be as tall as a double-decker bus!

It took gigantic steps that were as long as a small car.

jaw

leg

Tyrannosaurus rex
(tie-RAN-owe-SORE-uss-REX)

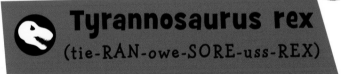

- lived around 67-65 million years ago
- 13 ft (4 m) tall

Parasaurolophus

Parasaurolophus had a long **crest** that stuck out from its head like a **snorkel**! It would walk on all-fours when it was eating, but would switch to two legs when it needed a quick escape.

tail

long back leg

foot

crest

Mad about parasaurolophus

Parasaurolophus had side teeth, but no teeth in the front of its mouth. As teeth wore out, new ones grew to replace them.

The crest on its head could grow up to 6 ft (1.8 m) long!

Hooting horn

Parasaurolophus's long crest was actually a hollow, bony **horn** that it may have used to make loud, **hooting sounds**.

head

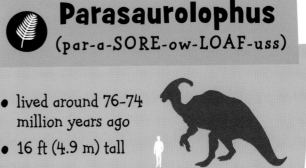

Parasaurolophus
(par-a-SORE-ow-LOAF-uss)

- lived around 76-74 million years ago
- 16 ft (4.9 m) tall

Brachiosaurus

Brachiosaurus was a giant eating machine! Its **arms** were longer than its **back legs**, so its body sloped down towards its tail. Like other dinosaurs, even the huge **brachiosaurus** hatched from an egg.

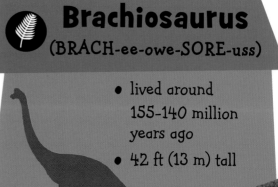

Brachiosaurus
(BRACH-ee-owe-SORE-uss)

- lived around 155-140 million years ago
- 42 ft (13 m) tall

tail......

Giant dinosaurs

Apatosaurus (brontosaurus) also had a long neck and tail like **brachiosaurus**.

back leg

Taller than T rex

Brachiosaurus could raise its head up to 42 ft (13 m) off the ground—that's over twice the height of **T rex**.

long neck

arm

Mad about brachiosaurus

Brachiosaurus was one of the heaviest dinosaurs. It could weigh over 70 tons (63,500 kg), or more than 30 cars!

Its neck was twice as long as a giraffe's!

Brachiosaurus had scary, chisel-like teeth, but fortunately it only ate plants.

It was a big eater, eating up to 440 lb (200 kg) of food a day. That's like eating 200 cabbages!

Allosaurus

Allosaurus was a terrifying **meat eater** that existed way before T rex. It had a massive **jaw** and **sharp claws** on its three-fingered hands.

Mad about allosaurus

Allosaurus could open its mouth wide enough to swallow an adult pig in one gulp.

Its short arms ended in daggerlike claws. Allosaurus used these claws to tear up its victims.

It had two horns that shaded its eyes from the sun—like a pair of sunglasses!

sharp claw

tail

Shapely teeth

Allosaurus had about 40 long, sharp **teeth** with **sawlike** edges. Its teeth curved backwards to stop its victims from escaping.

teeth

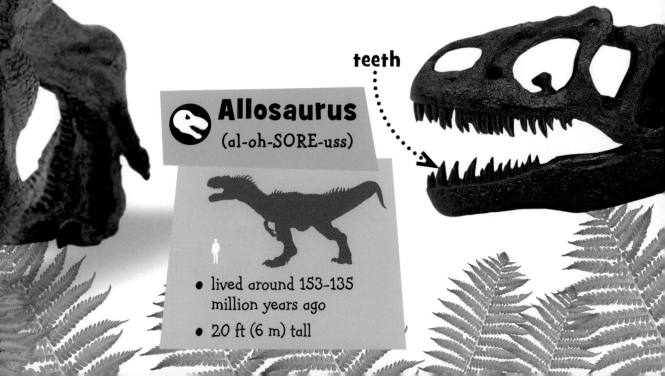

Allosaurus
(al-oh-SORE-uss)

- lived around 153–135 million years ago
- 20 ft (6 m) tall

Dino fun!

Use your stickers to have some d

Dinosaurs

Use these stickers to make your dinosaur scene!

Spinosaurus

Spinosaurus was one of the largest **meat-eating** dinosaurs ever—even bigger than **T rex**. With massive **spines** sticking out of its back, it looked terrifying!

Spinosaurus
(SPY-no-SORE-uss)

- lived around 125-95 million years ago
- 18.5 ft (5.6 m) tall

spines

tail

Mad about spinosaurus

Spinosaurus had a long crocodile-like snout that was great for catching and eating fish.

The bony spines on its back could be as tall as 6 ft (2 m). That's taller than most adults!

Warm up!

The **spines** on **spinosaurus**'s back were called a "**sail**." When the sail turned towards the sun, it helped spinosaurus to **warm up** quickly.

sail

crocodile-like snout

stegosaurus

Stegosaurus had
large, tough **plates**
on its back and sharp
spikes on its tail. The
spikes helped protect
it from attackers.

head............

Stegosaurus
(STEG-owe-SORE-uss)

- lived around 155-144
  million years ago
- 13 ft (4 m) tall

plate

foot

plate

Mad about stegosaurus

Some scientists think stegosaurus used its plates to impress other stegosauruses— the big show off!

As it chewed, stegosaurus stored food in its cheeks rather like a hamster.

Although its brain was tiny, some scientists think stegosaurus had another brain in its tail!

spike

leg

Tiny brain

Stegosaurus was the size of a bus, but its brain was only the size of a walnut.

its brain would be in here

Triceratops

Triceratops was a strong, **plant-eating** dinosaur with three **horns** and a bony **frill** on its head. Its sharp horns looked fierce but it probably used them to show off to other dinosaurs.

tail

Birdlike beak

Triceratops had a mouth shaped like a bird's **beak**. It used this to pluck out food.

beak

frill

Mad about triceratops

Triceratops could weigh as much as two big elephants.

Its huge head was filled with up to 800 sharp teeth! An average human only has 32!

Triceratops means "three-horned face."

horn

Triceratops
(try-SERRA-tops)

- lived around 68–65 million years ago
- 10 ft (3 m) tall

Velociraptor

Velociraptor was armed with a terrifying, **sharp claw** on the second toe of each **foot**. Scientists think that **velociraptor** used its claws to grab hold of its victims and climb over them.

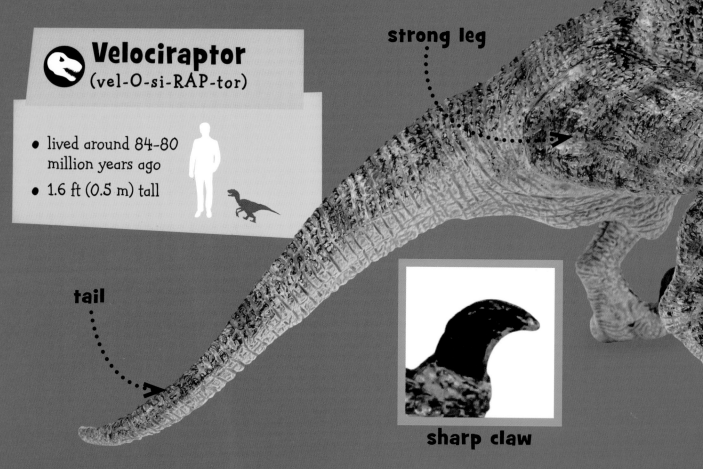

Velociraptor
(vel-O-si-RAP-tor)

- lived around 84-80 million years ago
- 1.6 ft (0.5 m) tall

strong leg

tail

sharp claw

Toothy jaw

Velociraptor had a narrow **jaw** with about 80 sharp, pointed **teeth.** It used the teeth to tear into just about anything.

Mad about velociraptors

Velociraptor was super speedy. Over short distances, it could run as fast as an Olympic sprinter!

The sharp claws on velociraptor's feet were nearly 2.5 in (6.5 cm) long. That's over half the width of this page!

Velociraptors were smart dinosaurs, hunting for their prey in groups.

Scientists think that velociraptor may have been covered with hair and feathers.

narrow jaw

sharp teeth

Guess who?

Look at the pictures, read the clues, and guess the dinosaurs!

1

I have a big, spiny "sail" sticking out of my back.

2

I'm as big as a bus, but my brain is only the size of a walnut.

3

I have three horns and a big, bony frill on my head. I eat plants.

4

I am very heavy and my neck is twice as long as a giraffe's.

5

I use my long, bony crest to make loud hooting sounds.

6

I have a large, curved claw on the second toe of each foot.